C. G

My Chair

Written by Betsy James

Illustrated by Mary Newell DePalma

Arthur A. Levine Books · An Imprint of Scholastic Inc.

For Maura, Tim, Kevin, Bridget, and the newest Newell —M.N.D.

For Mary, who started it all —B.J.

Text copyright © 2004 by Betsy James / Illustrations copyright © 2004 by Mary Newell DePalma

James, Betsy.
My chair / by Betsy James ; illustrated by Mary Newell DePalma.   1st ed.   p. cm.
Summary: A group of children celebrate their various chairs and their imaginations as they gather to welcome a new neighbor.
ISBN 0-439-44421-7
[1. Chairs—Fiction. 2. Neighbors—Fiction.] I. DePalma, Mary Newell, ill. II. Title.
PZ7.J15357My 2004   [E]—dc21   2003003934
1 3 5 7 9 10 8 6 4 2   04 05 06 07 08

The text font for this book was set in Chauncy, designed by Chank Diesel.
The display font was set in Dartangnon ITC.
The art for this book was created using acrylics.
Book design by Elizabeth B. Parisi and Mary Newell DePalma

Printed in Singapore 46 · First edition, July 2004

Bring your chair.
Put it there.

My chair works
because I bend
in the middle.

My chair holds me up in the air.

It gets my bottom
up off the ground
so nothing can bite it,
like a spider
or a mouse.

My chair makes me tall.
It keeps my ice cream
higher than the dog.

My chair clacks and skreaks.

It has elbows
and pointy knees,
and it folds up.
It's light as
a tumbleweed.

My chair is squishy. It eats people.

It eats quarters and trucks
and colored pencils and my arm
and my leg and my brother
and my bicycle.
It has pockets in its cheeks
like a chipmunk.

My chair smells good...

...because it used to be
a tree.

Who does not use chairs?

Birds, fish, skunks, pigs, weasels –

everybody but us.

My chair rocks.
Mine rolls.

Most chairs just sit there,
but mine's more like a horse or a train.
It's not quite legs, and not quite wings....
It's like glasses —
I put it on in the morning.
I wear my chair
to zoom like a roller skater,
dance like a bear.

My chair is a fort,

a forest,
a tower,

a truck, a gate,
a cage,
an ocean,

a ship, a plane,
a prison,

an intergalactic zoo.

In my chair
I consider what's fair.

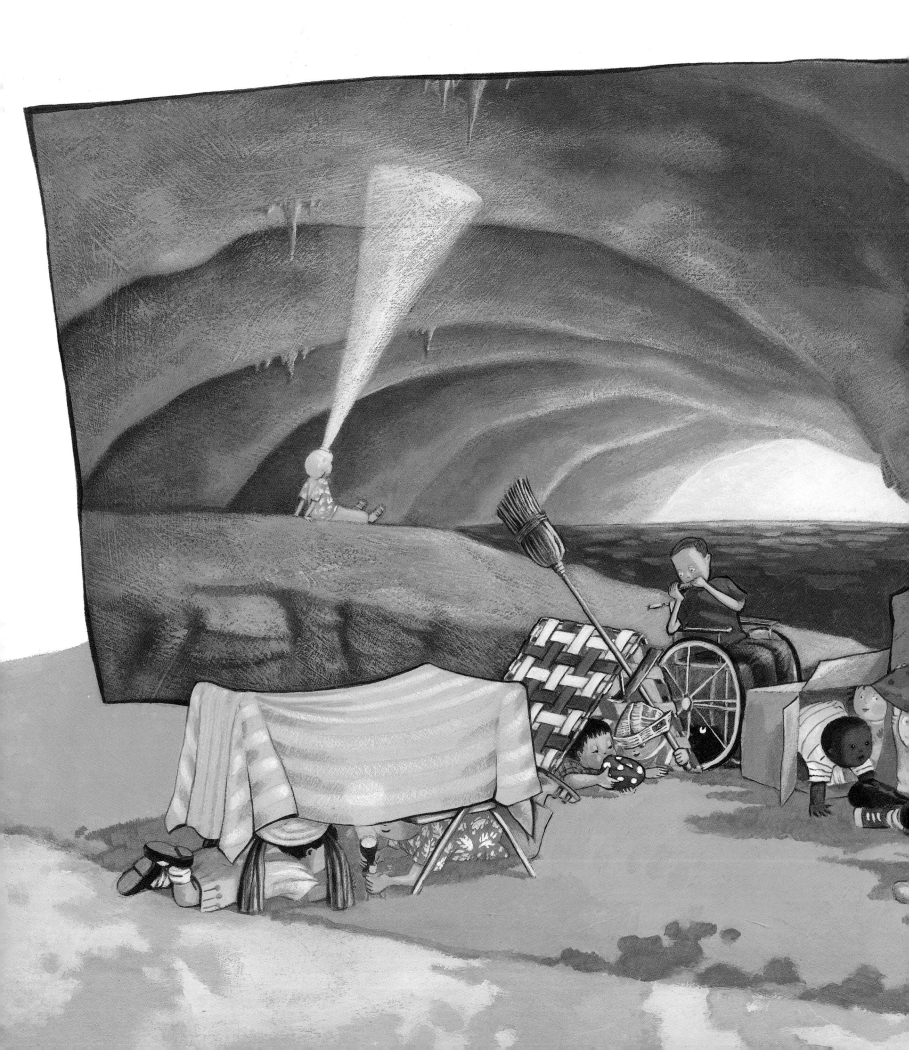

Underneath my chair
is a place where grown-ups aren't.
Underneath my chair are
all the caves in the world,
all the darkness,
and the safest treasure.

When the world is too big,
my chair is just right.

When my chair is too big,
I crawl under it,
and there is the right size room
with windows.

My chair is for me.

My chair is here.

My chair is home.